For all the Grandmas and Grandpas who broke their backs working in the fields so we wouldn't have to

BLOOMSBURY CHILDREN'S BOOKS
Bloomsbury Publishing Inc., part of Bloomsbury Publishing Plc
1385 Broadway, New York, NY 10018

BLOOMSBURY, BLOOMSBURY CHILDREN'S BOOKS, and the Diana logo are trademarks of Bloomsbury Publishing Plc

First published in the United States of America in May 2019
by Bloomsbury Children's Books

Text and illustrations copyright © 2019 by Elizabeth Zunon

Bloomsbury books may be purchased for business or promotional use. For information on bulk purchases please contact Macmillan Corporate and Premium Sales Department at specialmarkets@macmillan.com

Library of Congress Cataloging-in-Publication Data
Names: Zunon, Elizabeth, author, illustrator.
Title: Grandpa Cacao / by Elizabeth Zunon.
Description: New York : Bloomsbury, 2019.
Summary: As a little girl and her father work together to make her birthday cake, he tells the story of her Grandpa Cacao,
a farmer from the Ivory Coast. Includes author's note and a cake recipe.
Identifiers: LCCN 2018045160 (print) • LCCN 2018051273 (e-book)
ISBN 978-1-68119-640-4 (hardcover) • ISBN 978-1-68119-641-1 (e-book) • ISBN 978-1-68119-642-8 (e-PDF)
Subjects: | CYAC: Cacao—Fiction. | Cake—Fiction. | Family life—Fiction. | African Americans—Fiction.
Classification: LCC PZ7.1.Z87 Gr 2019 (print) | LCC PZ7.1.Z87 (e-book) | DDC [E]—dc23
LC record available at https://lccn.loc.gov/2018045160

Art created with oil paint and collage with screen print
Typeset in Warugaki, Luckiest Guy, and LinoLetter
Book design by John Candell
Printed in China by Leo Paper Products, Heshan, Guangdong
2 4 6 8 10 9 7 5 3 1

All papers used by Bloomsbury Publishing Plc are natural, recyclable products made from wood grown in well-managed forests.
The manufacturing processes conform to the environmental regulations of the country of origin.

To find out more about our authors and books visit www.bloomsbury.com and sign up for our newsletters.

# GRANDPA CACAO

## A TALE OF CHOCOLATE, FROM FARM TO FAMILY

### WRITTEN AND ILLUSTRATED BY
# ELIZABETH ZUNON

BLOOMSBURY
CHILDREN'S BOOKS
NEW YORK  LONDON  OXFORD  NEW DELHI  SYDNEY

Chocolate is my most favorite thing *ever*. For my birthday, Daddy and I are making our family's special celebration cake while Mommy goes to pick up another treat.

Every one of us loves this cake. Even my little brother, Denny, who is the pickiest of picky eaters.

"Chocolate is a gift to you from Grandpa Cacao," Daddy says. "We can only enjoy chocolate treats thanks to farmers like him."

I've never met Grandpa Cacao, but I've heard his voice on the phone. I can almost picture him: a mystery from Africa, a place I've never been.

"Tell me again about Grandpa Cacao," I ask. "Are you like him? Am I?"

"We're from a land called the Ivory Coast,"
Daddy says, "where I grew up watching big, graceful
elephants roam. It's where the air breathes hot and
damp, thick with stories and music and the languages
of people from tiny villages and big cities. Grandpa
Cacao's farm was the pride of his life."

"The air, the rain, and the soil must be just right for growing cacao." Daddy holds a sieve over the mixing bowl, and I pour in the flour. "Grandpa Cacao carried heavy loads through the bush, back and forth to his fields on his wide, calloused feet."

"That must be where I get my wide-boat feet!" I say as I add the baking powder.

"Your Grandpa Cacao spotted the ripe fruits ready to be picked from the forest canopy and cut them right off the tree trunks quickly and precisely."

*Just like the way I can spot the end of summer from tinges of orange at the tips of treetops!*

"He sliced through the skins of the pods without cutting into any of the sticky white beans inside." I carefully sprinkle in the salt. "Grandpa Cacao could hold two, or even three whole fruits in one of his rough hands . . ."

"Like a giant! Did you ever help?" I ask.

"Everybody in the village worked together," says Daddy, as he melts the chocolate and butter. "When I turned seven, Grandma let me help gather and scoop out the cacao pods, but only if my schoolwork and chores were done!"

"Grandpa Cacao and the other villagers scooped out millions of cacao beans and put them in big pits in the ground lined with banana leaves. They stirred the cacao beans every few days until they changed from white to light brown. Then Grandpa Cacao and the other strong men hoisted the beans out of the pits and onto a cement floor under the sun to dry. Warm whiffs of chocolate wafted through the air!"

"We lugged the beans inside every single night so they wouldn't rot in the morning dew," says Daddy. "If tropical storm clouds rolled in, we all rushed to cover up the drying beans so that the mighty rains wouldn't drench them!"

*I bet he could smell the rain a mile away, the way I can smell a cold day!*

"When the skins of the dried beans made a *crak-crak*-cracking sound between your fingers, they were ready to sell," says Daddy.

"Did they taste like chocolate?" I ask. My stomach is grumbling. I wonder what Mommy is bringing home.

"They tasted bitter but always left a sweetness on the tongue." He adds the sugar to our cake batter.

"*Crak...crack...crak...*" I break one, two, three eggs into the bowl but don't let any shells fall in. Daddy mixes as I pour in the milk.

"Once I got older," says Daddy, "I helped your Grandpa Cacao bag up the beans to sell to the cacao buyers. If the roads weren't flooded from the rains, they came to our village in trucks with their big scales and bundles of money to buy our beans, then they sent them off for chocolate making."

"Once we sold our cacao beans, we dashed off to the Friday market. It buzzed with every farmer in town eager to spend his hard-earned money!" Daddy smiles as he remembers. "We used our money to buy food, school supplies, uniforms, books, and fabric to have our special occasion clothes made. Your Grandpa Cacao and I always visited Grandma's fruit stall at the market with a surprise."

I take over the mixing while
Daddy greases the cake pan. I'm
wondering if it's a new party dress
that Mommy's gone to get me.

"You know, you're a lot like your Grandpa Cacao!" This makes us both smile. The batter smells more and more chocolaty! I'm getting so hungry. I wonder if Mommy's gone to pick up that puppy I've been wishing for!

"Grandpa Cacao didn't eat anything chocolate himself," says Daddy, "because it was a fancy and expensive treat. But the kids couldn't resist sneaking a taste of the pulp from the cacao fruits or the candy-sweet drink we made from it."

Daddy dips a finger into the bowl and has a taste: "*Mmmm . . .* candy-sweet!" He hands me the wooden spoon and I start to mix again, but my arms get tired fast. I help by licking the spoon.

"Almost done!" says Daddy as he pours the thick, gooey batter into the greased cake pan like a chocolate waterfall! I scrape the last of it in and think about Grandpa Cacao and all that he did to help make this cake.

Daddy pops the pan into the oven and we wait . . .
The batter rises and slowly bakes. I can smell the chocolaty-ness
oozing from the oven, and I can't wait to taste it!

As I help wipe the counters, the doorbell rings and the oven timer goes off: *"My cake is baked!! Mommy's home!! Get the forks!!!"* I yell.

I run to the front door.

Mommy walks in with a hunched-over man I've never seen.

"Happy birthday!" he says to me with an accent that sounds like Daddy's . . . in that voice I've heard on the phone. He's an old man, the same color as me. He's got my same small ears and Daddy's smile, and he looks at me like he's known me forever.

He pulls me into a strong hug, then offers me a big, oval fruit that's yellowish orange. I can feel how rough his hands are as I take it from him. I need both my hands to hold the fruit. "Your birthday present," he says.

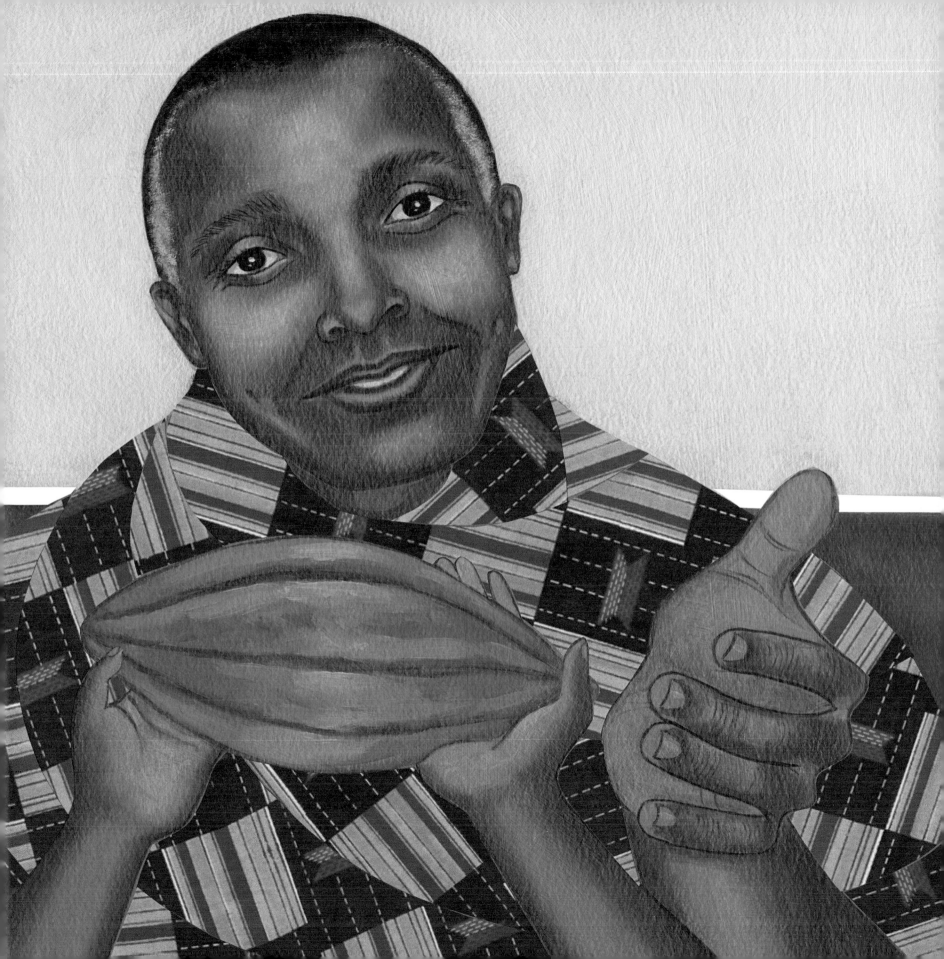

I recognize his twinkling eyes, and I know: HE is my Grandpa Cacao—the *best* birthday present *ever* in the world!

# AUTHOR'S NOTE

I spent my childhood in Abidjan, the biggest city in the Ivory Coast. I never saw a cacao tree in real life, but my father told me stories of visiting his father's plantation up in the country as a little boy. His stories, as well as the fact that I never met my own Grandpa Cacao, were the inspiration for this book. I hope to one day return to the Ivory Coast, walk through a real cacao plantation, and hold a real cacao pod in my hand.

"**Cacao**" is the word used for the tree and the fruit; it is believed to come from a Mayan word. The Mayans referred to cacao as "god food."

"**Cocoa**" is the word used for the products made from the fruits of the cacao tree, like cocoa powder, which is made in a factory. Cocoa powder can be found in chocolate cakes, chocolate milk, and chocolate bars.

### THE REALITIES OF THE CACAO TRADE

In recent years, we've heard many stories about child labor in the cacao industry. While some children help out on family farms, there is also a long history of exploitation, which goes back to the colonial era of forced labor. There is a current effort by the big candy companies to ensure that the cacao they buy doesn't come from farms where child or slave labor is used. The government of the Ivory Coast is also trying to clamp down on such practices.

### WHAT YOU CAN DO

As a consumer, you can look for chocolate that is certified as **Fair Trade**, meaning that it was harvested without child or slave labor, and that the cacao farmer received a fair price for his or her beans.

# THE ART

To tell Grandpa Cacao's story and the little girl's story simultaneously on the same page, I needed to use two different art techniques that would be complementary to each other yet exist on their own . . . like quality ingredients that combine to make a scrumptious cake! Depicting Grandpa Cacao and the people in his world in flat, opaque screen-printed shapes shows how he exists in the little girl's imagination as an almost mythical figure. I painted the tropical backgrounds of Grandpa Cacao's world in Africa and the contemporary scenes in oil paint on watercolor paper, using some collaged elements in the contemporary scenes as well. Then, I painted each Grandpa Cacao work scene on a silk screen of its own and screen-printed it onto its corresponding painted background, and *voilà!* The two worlds became one!

# CHOCOLATE CHUNKS

## SCIENCE

The chocolate we eat all around the world comes from cacao trees that grow only in tropical climates near the equator. The Ivory Coast provided 45 percent of the world's cacao until recently. Ghana, Indonesia, Mexico, and Hawai'i also have the perfect hot, wet climate for growing cacao trees.

## HISTORY

The first people in the world to ever eat or drink chocolate were the ancient Maya and Aztecs in what is today Mexico and Guatemala. It is believed that Mayan gods ate the fruits of the cacao tree. The Aztecs worshipped a god named Quetzalcoatl, who they believed brought the seeds of the cacao tree from the Garden of Life to give to humans. The cacao bean was precious to the Aztecs; they used it to make a special drink called *chocolatl* for important people like Emperor Montezuma. The cacao beans were even used as money!

# FROM BEAN TO TREAT

"I helped your Grandpa Cacao bag up the beans to sell to the cacao buyers. If the roads were good, they came to our village in trucks with their big scales and bundles of money to buy our beans, then they sent them off for chocolate making."

Once cacao bean shipments arrive at chocolate factories, mostly in Europe or America, workers empty the big sacks of beans into round rotating ovens where they are roasted. Then, they take a trip on a conveyor belt to a winnowing machine

that cracks open the cacao beans to remove their hard, bitter shells and reveals the center, or nib, of the beans.

Next, the cacao beans travel down another conveyor belt to the mixer, whose big heavy wheels grind and mash them into a thick paste, called chocolate liquor. Cocoa butter is removed from some of the liquor, which is then crushed into powder and packaged. This cocoa powder will be sold to make chocolate treats.

The rest of the chocolate liquor will be turned into chocolate bars. Workers add sugar and vanilla flavoring to sweeten the chocolate, and extra cocoa butter to help make it smooth and silky. All these ingredients are mixed together until they are turned into a coarse paste that is poured into a vat with a metal roller, which grinds the chocolate paste from gritty to smooth.

Finally, the chocolate is poured into another mixer, where it is tempered. This machine heats, mixes, and cools the chocolate until it is smooth and shiny. It is then squirted into molds where it cools and hardens into chocolate bars! The chocolate bars are then wrapped in paper, packed in boxes, and sent to stores all over the world, where you and I can buy them!

# CHOCOLATE CELEBRATION CAKE RECIPE

Let the butter and eggs come to room temperature before you begin.

Preheat the oven to 350 degrees Fahrenheit.

This recipe makes one 9-inch cake layer.

*SIFT TOGETHER INTO A LARGE BOWL:*

  1¼ cups all-purpose flour

  2 teaspoons baking powder

*THEN ADD:*

  ¼ teaspoon salt

*IN A SEPARATE BOWL, MELT TOGETHER IN THE MICROWAVE USING 20-SECOND INCREMENTS:*

  4 ounces semi-sweet baking chocolate

  ½ cup unsalted butter

*ADD TO CHOCOLATE MIXTURE:*

  ¾ cup packed dark brown sugar

  ¼ cup granulated white sugar

*BEAT WELL. THEN, WHISK IN UNTIL LIQUIDY AND SHINY LIKE CHOCOLATE SYRUP:*

  3 eggs

  ¼ cup milk

  *If you're feeling adventurous, add some cinnamon or chili powder like the ancient Aztecs did to their drinking chocolate!*

*POUR THE CHOCOLATE MIXTURE INTO THE FLOUR MIXTURE AND MIX UNTIL JUST COMBINED.*

Pour into a 9-inch round greased cake pan and bake for 30 minutes. Remove from oven, and let cool before adding chocolate frosting, fruit slices, or any other cake toppings you like!

For a special snowflake decoration, place a paper snowflake on the baked cake and sprinkle the top with confectioners' sugar. Carefully remove the snowflake by picking it straight up off the cake, and **voilà!** A snowflake cake!